THE SOLUTION

By

Rick McQuiston

PHASE 5
PHASE 5 PUBLISHING, LLC
PO BOX 3131
ASHEVILLE, NC 28802
WWW.PHASE5PUBLISHING.COM

First Edition October 2014
Copyright 2014 Phase 5 Publishing, LLC
Story Copyright 2012 by Rick McQuiston, Licensed to
Phase 5 Publishing, LLC
Cover art, *Undead Horizon,* Copyright 2013 by Dylan
Hansen, Licensed to Phase 5 Publishing, LLC
Interior art used with appropriate permissions and
licensing, see Image Credits after About the Author for
listing

Horror. Vampires, other dimensions, forbidden
knowledge, supernatural, evil object, reality manipulation,
invasion, speculative fiction, things man was not meant to
know.

Teen and Adult readers: Non-graphic violence and death,
evil object, addiction, unromantic vampires.

ISBN 978-0-9835795-7-1 $8.99 Contains art not included
in E-book edition
E-book ISBN 978-0-9835795-6-4 $3.95

Printed and Distributed by Lightning Source, a member of
the Ingram Content Group, in the United States of America

The Solution

Prologue

The newscaster seemed agitated as she addressed the camera. Her curly brown hair was tangled with tree twigs and her mascara was blotted around her eyes, giving her a strange gothic look. Her clothes were dirty and tattered, as if she had been in some scuffle. She had obviously not slept in days, and her exhaustion was clear.

"There have been numerous reports from all over the country concerning people, whom some are describing as a type of vampire, having overrun nearly everything in their path.

"These creatures have been reported in areas ranging from rural farmlands to major metropolitan cities. They have been seen in lands as far north as the Northern Territories of Canada and seem to be spreading without regard for human or animal life. The federal government has issued a state of emergency for…a state of emergency-" her eyes widened and all the blood drained from her face.

Suddenly her head was lopped cleanly off her shoulders. The chalk-white creature standing directly behind her scowled in triumph at his conquest, his grotesque face splattered with blood, sinews straining at his skin, eyes burning like a nightmare as he looked at the camera. He lunged and the camera canted sideways, the screen went dark.

1

Brad pushed the little girl back, shielding her from the flying jagged glass. He knew the windows would not keep them out. He also knew the crucifixes would only have a minimal effect, if any at all. One needed faith for them work, and he could not lie to himself about the strength of his.

Brad grabbed the little girl, tossed her over his shoulder, and darted towards the library at the far end of the hallway. He ignored the bleeding gash in his leg.

The man who lived in the house had obviously believed in the supernatural; the crucifixes and various religious artifacts filling the walls attested strongly to that. Brad could only pray that he had wooden stakes or something, anything that would stop the bloodsucking nightmares that had overrun the country.

Breathing a sigh of relief, Brad slammed the heavy wrought iron door shut behind them, sliding a thick metal bar across and into its slot. He leaned up against the door as if hearing their approach might delay their pursuit somehow. He knew vampires feared wrought iron; clearly the owner of the house did as well.

Brad's mind wondered briefly about the whereabouts of the owner. He was not here, in this sanctuary, perhaps he fled elsewhere. Brad had not noted any signs of blood or bodies anywhere else in the house, so he assumed the man had made it out safely.

The little girl seemed remarkably calm given the dangerous and frightening circumstances, and seated herself behind the large oak desk that dominated the room. Her long black hair reflected the moonlight cascading down from the series of small, round skylights high in the ceiling. It gave her a somewhat mysterious look he found disturbing on one so young.

She said not a word and showed no indication of fear or worry. Hundreds, if not thousands, of vicious, bloodthirsty vampires trying to get to them and not a trace of panic on a girl of no more than six years old. Brad still felt compelled to console her. He had lost his little sister, and in an odd sort of way he felt a connection to this strange little girl.

"Are you okay, honey?" Brad whispered. The air in the room was thick with stagnation. "What's your name?"

The little girl looked up from the desktop. Saying nothing, she peered past Brad's shoulder at the heavy iron door. Her eyes were locked onto it; Brad's words seemed to flutter past her attention like butterflies on a bright, sunny day.

"Honey," Brad asked while trying to keep his expression calm. "Are you hurt? Do you have any injuries?"

Only silence filled the room. Brad's

attention followed the little girl's vacant stare over to the door and the incredible carvings covering it. His eyes widened at the plump devils reveling within seething cauldrons, the leering demons feasting upon decayed human body parts, swirling storms punctuated by angry jolts of twisted lightening and dancing imps surrounding screaming victims, prodding them with enormous, bloody pitchforks. Such wicked images, so masterfully etched upon the wrought iron canvas of the door, disturbed him.

Brad took a careful step toward the door and its obscene tableau. He could not explain why it frightened him so deeply, almost as much as the vampires frightened him. Perhaps it was knowing that such a magnificent and equally monstrous door was the only obstacle between them and certain death.

Brad turned his back to horrific masterpiece and stared at the little girl. He wanted to ask her if she knew anything about what was happening, but restrained himself from doing so. He had a nagging suspicion that she knew something, something important, but she *was* only a child, albeit a strange one. Surely she had no idea what was going on. He crept away from the nightmarish door to the front of the desk. He looked into her large eyes and searched for any indication of pain, anything that would help him understand her or their situation.

"Are you okay, honey?" he asked for what

felt like the hundredth time. "I know you've seen some pretty scary stuff lately. I sure know I have, and I would guess there's probably more to come, but if we stick together and help each other out, maybe, just maybe, we can figure a way out."

Any hope he had for a response was quickly dashed. The little girl merely continued to stare at the door, their only barrier between life and death.

Frustrated and desperate, Brad threw his arms up in defeat. "Fine. You don't wanna talk, we won't talk. I was just hoping you could tell me something to help us out."

He instantly felt guilty for his outburst. He did not want to frighten the poor little thing any more than she probably already was. But his patience was running out, as was their time. He had other problems to deal with at the moment, such as preparing for when the vampires would find them.

He looked around the room for anything he could move against the door for added support. The skylights were the only windows in the room, for which Brad was extremely grateful. The walls were covered by thick, sturdy bookshelves, lined from top to bottom with a large variety of tomes of every size and color.

A suspicion entered Brad's mind and refused to fade. Brad walked over to one of the smaller shelves, wedged his fingers behind it as much as he could and pulled.

It moved, but only three or four inches. Brad leaned in as far as he could and peered at the wall. Just as he suspected, it was made of wrought iron.

2

Brad awoke to a headache unlike any he had ever experienced before. He attributed it to the combination of hunger, thirst, exhaustion and fear. His experiences these last few weeks could fill a book. He had lost everyone he had ever cared about and, he feared, more than a small part of himself.

Brad had managed to survive because he was quick and he could think on his feet. He stayed on the move, always watching, never letting himself get cornered. He never left any traces of his whereabouts or clues which might help them track him. Yet the vampires had taken a part of him that could never be replaced, leaving a hole that festered and could never be filled. There was no going back to the way things were before. Even if those terrible creatures simply vanished into thin air, the memories would linger far longer than any man could possibly endure. Insanity would forever be tapping on the fragile barrier of his mind.

Brad looked over at the little girl, who was asleep with her head on the massive desk. Her tiny arms were splayed out on either side of her, and her dirty blond hair obscured most of her face. She reminded Brad of a statue he had once admired in a church.

The sound was small at first, nearly inaudible, but it was there nonetheless.

Scratching.

Light, almost gentle scratching emanating from the other side of the door. It sounded like someone, or some*thing*, was exploring the impediment to its next meal, testing the structure for any weaknesses.

Brad's heart was in his throat. He knew they would be done for if the vampires breached the door and gained access to the room. He knew he had survived so far partially because he always thought one step ahead of the creatures. He anticipated their next move. Now he knew what would happen if he could not find a weapon, or a way to exit the house without being seen.

The vampires' cunning and intelligence were matched only by their savagery. It was as if the greater their numbers, the more strategic and organized they became. Their complex and carefully planned attacks overtook people by the thousands, decimating whole cites, entire countries in a matter of weeks. Different militaries from across the world tried numerous strategies against them, but only succeeded in delaying their own demise. Their training and tactics had simply never even contemplated such an enemy. It became painfully apparent early on that the world just was not prepared to deal with the vampires on any level.

Brad carefully, quietly, crawled over to the door and rested his ear on it. At first he heard nothing more than the scratching noises, but then-

Whispers.

Thin, growling murmurs, barely suppressed, sounded as if they were about to burst out at full volume any moment. Brad backed away from the door. Something in his gut, fostered by his many terrible experiences, warned him not to get too close.

And then all hell broke loose on the other side of the door.

The vampires had sensed, or smelled, someone inside the room and their lust for blood erupted with such terrible intensity that Brad fell backwards onto his rear end in a reflexive move to get away from the noise.

He watched in disbelief as the door was assaulted so violently it bent inward slightly, straining at the heavy iron hinges. His eyes and mind searched for a way out. Leaning back, he looked over his shoulder at the little girl who was now wide awake and staring at him. His desperation overrode his concern for her.

"You have to tell me if you know anything. Where to find a weapon. Or a way out. Please. Our lives depend on it."

The pandemonium on the other side of the door grew louder. They were fighting with each other to get at the door, smashing their powerful fists into it continuously. With each terrible hit the door bent minutely. With each deformation the iron wailed a metallic cry of pain and resistance. The creatures' assault on the door and each other intensified, creating a chorus of ear-splitting horror. Within a minute huge dents littered the face of it, some looking as if they would rupture with one more hit.

"Please, do you know how to stop this? Can you help me stop this?"

She continued to stare at him, either ignoring or not understanding his words.

"What's your name? Do you live here? Where are your parents?" Brad had to restrain himself from losing his temper again. This was definitely not the time for it, and it would only make matters worse.

Maybe she was in shock. Perhaps she had suffered some injury to the head, or was just born with some type of mental deficiency. She appeared to be in perfect health. No fever, no bruises, no bleeding, nothing.

Brad wondered just how much longer the door would hold. Maybe another hour, maybe only another minute. Either way it did not matter unless he could find some solution. And then it occurred to him.

What if there isn't one?

3

Brad found himself slipping away from this awful moment. He had survived so much for so long that the idea he might actually be at the end of the line just would not completely register. He began to feel even more helpless than when he first witnessed the vampires' attack. He could never forget the poor teenage girl who was so swiftly dispatched by the creatures. She never even knew what hit her.

So young. So innocent. And to perish in such a violent and bloody manner.

Brad had little in the way of family. His mother had passed away when he was just a toddler, and left him with only his alcoholic father and his little sister, Amy.

Amy. She was so beautiful and smart, and such a pretty name too. Brad had always been very close to her, consoling her when she was down, spending time with her whenever he could, and generally being like a father to her. He felt someone should take care of her, since their real father cared more for his whiskey and vodka than his own kids.

The memory of her death stung Brad like a hot needle, probing with its sharp tip, grinding its point into his very heart and soul.

"Brad, help me," Amy had cried as two vampires dragged her kicking and screaming through her bedroom window. "Braaad!"

Brad ran into her bedroom when he heard

her scream, but only got there in time to see his little sister being pulled away to her doom. He had tried before to talk her out of keeping her bed directly underneath her window. He should have made her listen.

Not that it would really have made a difference.

His name was the last word he heard her say. He thought it poetic that her final word was his name, the person who loved her most, the one who had tried so hard to give her something close to a normal family life.

But I failed her when it really mattered. He felt guilty for not jumping through the window and chasing after her, but the shock and utter helplessness had crippled him completely. He told himself he could not have caught the vampires anyway, they were much too fast. Within a few seconds they had been nearly out of sight. And even if he had caught them, what then?

4

The door was holding up very well, considering the vampires' onslaught. Brad shuddered when he thought of what must be happening on the other side of the door. He had seen their ferocity and power first hand. Even wrought iron did little to deter them, if they were hungry or angry enough. Their need and rage would overcome their fear, eventually they would find a way to get through, indifferent to their own safety.

Brad was surprised when the little girl abruptly stood up from behind the desk and walked over to where he stood. Her eyes conveyed pity as well as a sense of confidence. She seemed oblivious to the thrashing the door was taking from the vampires, and focused directly on Brad.

Now that he had her attention, his desperation insisted he get her to speak. "Do you know what is going on here?"

"My name is...." She paused, seating herself on the floor. "My name is... actually, I am not quite sure what my name is, or if I ever had one at all." A tear welled in her eye. "If I ever had one at all."

Any fear that was crippling Brad's thoughts melted away.

"I know you're probably frightened. I am, but we have to try and find a way out of this mess." He waited for a reaction from her.

Nothing. "Listen to me. That door probably won't hold too much longer, not with the way those things are attacking it. If there is anything that you're not telling me, anything at all, please say it. Maybe it can help us somehow."

The little girl wiped her tears away and thought for a moment. "Follow me," she said with a hint of a smile.

Brad eagerly trailed behind her, his hope for survival reviving slightly.

She sauntered casually over to the enormous oak desk in the center of the room. She reached down, pushed her dark hair out of her face, opened the lower left drawer. Brad resisted crowding her. Apparently she knew exactly what she was looking for. Now that she was doing something, he was not going to hinder her in any way.

She clamped both her tiny hands around a large, faded red book and withdrew it from the drawer. It was at least three inches thick and tightly bound with a heavy iron clasp, like nothing he had ever seen before. All he could determine was that it seemed old and odd. She plopped it down onto the desktop with a heavy thud and looked up at Brad.

"This might be of some help to you," she muttered. "I'm not sure where you need to look, but the answers you seek are contained within it."

Brad noted she had a strange grasp of language for someone so young. "I'll see what I can find," he announced with what little confidence he had left.

"But please hurry," the little girl warned as she glanced over at the door. "We haven't much time."

Now she notices, he thought, then pushed his annoyance aside in favor of finding something—anything—that might give them an edge when the living nightmare breached the door.

Brad picked up the heavy tome and studied the clasp. It was a fairly simple mechanism, possibly unlocked with a key of some sort, and tarnished with streaks of rust. He flipped the book on its side and began to tap on the lock with his finger. Four tiny pinholes appeared out of nowhere, one on each side of the lock, and immediately started to flicker, as if they were fading in and out of existence.

"You must be quick. The openings are only visible for a few seconds, and then no more until another time, another time unknown to all."

Her words confused Brad, but he did not have time to figure her out right now. The vampires were attacking the door with more ferocity than ever, beating on it with their deformed white heads and filthy talons.

Brad felt helpless. What was he supposed to do?

"You'll need this," the little girl said as if reading his thoughts. She held up a small, unusual-looking device with four thin arms protruding from its edges. Brad took it from her and placed it squarely on top of the lock mechanism. The arms instantly clamped down on the book, locking into the four tiny holes. Then a heavy clicking sounded inside and Brad nearly shouted with joy. A few seconds later the device fell off to the side of the book, taking the lock mechanism along with it.

"You must hurry," the little girl reminded Brad. "You must be quick."

Brad flipped open the book and began scouring the delicate, yellowed pages.

5

Brad nearly vomited when he focused his attention on some of the pictures in the book: bloodied body parts, obese zombies rolling in human remains, laughing demons chucking screaming people into huge blazing pits. Brad tried to pass by the worst pages, but still had to at least look over them to some degree. He had no idea what he was searching for and could not afford to miss it, whatever it may be.

He rifled through the pages with the sounds of the voracious monsters smashing into the door ringing in his ears. Hunger was threatening to cripple him, as was thirst and just plain exhaustion, but he could not stop. Not now. He irrationally felt that possibly the future of mankind was involved, and he just might be the last chance. His grumbling and shrinking stomach and dry throat would just have to take a back seat. There were much more important things.

After seventy-five or eighty pages, Brad slammed his fist down in frustration. A drop of blood welled up beneath his palm, staining the desk and inflaming the vampires' attack on the door.

"How am I supposed to know what to look for?" he shouted. "How is a stupid book going to stop those things outside? What am I supposed to do?"

The little girl stared at him in puzzlement.

She brushed her hair from her face and sat back down at the desk.

"Don't let your fear overrule your determination. Continue your search. The solution will present itself to you in due time."

He almost longed for her silence again. "We don't have time for this! If you know something you have to tell me now!" Brad felt his emotions getting the better of his logic, and he feared completely losing his temper.

The little girl smiled at him. "I know you feel lost, but you must persevere. The fate of mankind might depend on it."

Girded by her validation of his desperate hope, Brad resumed looking through the pages of the book, hoping and praying he could find some useful information before it was too late. He concentrated as best as he could, trying to block out the terrible noise coming from behind the door. He began to babble while he flipped through the pages, struggled to maintain his composure, his sanity.

"Paaaage two-hundred forty-sevennnn," a gravelly voice screeched, the tone of a dentist's drill, high-pitched and full of promises of pain.

Brad's head snapped up from the book. His heart fell in his chest and the blood in his veins froze solid. Fear like he had never known gripped his mind.

The voice had come from the other side of the door.

6

The vampires were collecting in vast numbers. They roamed the countryside in packs of thousands, searching in an endless journey for food, death and destruction. For countless centuries they had waited, endured endless hardships and the suffering of their twisted, soulless bodies, frequently attempting to escape from their plight, always meeting with failure and pain. The phenomena that allowed their escape from their native plane was not understood, only exploited.

They did learn something from their near-endless torment: patience.

Patience allowed them to gather around the house where Brad and the little girl were hiding. It allowed them to study the building, its defenses and structural weaknesses. It allowed them to plan their attack and wait for just the right time to strike.

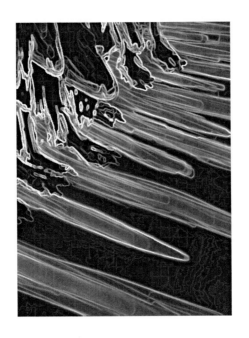

Despite all reason and caution, Brad felt compelled to listen to the voice and turn to page two-forty-seven of the book. The pages grew warmer as he flipped through them. He dismissed the observation as soon as it registered. *Just the exhaustion.*

Page two-forty-seven bore writing that was nearly illegible. The words were scrawled in thick black ink with swirls of bright red mingled freely throughout the text. Brad strained to decipher the writing, but only succeeded in frustrating himself further. It was apparently in some ancient language.

"I can't read this! This is hopeless." The notion of fighting his way past the vampires began to appear like an attractive alternative. This book, that door, this girl, that noise, it was just too much. He had fought them before and survived, he could do it again.

The little girl calmly stood and walked around the desk to where Brad stood. She grasped his hand, squeezed tightly, pulled it over to the open pages in the book.

"Feel your pain," she whispered to him. "Know the aches in your heart and use them as a portal to better things, to solutions for problems."

Brad felt anger rising up in his gut. "What does that mean?" he shouted at her. "Talk normal, not in riddles. We don't have time for games."

Her calm demeanor did not falter. "Use the anger and remorse you've experienced as a key. Only then will you be able to unlock doors and remove barricades."

Brad looked at her as a single tear rolled down his face. Maybe it was the exhaustion, but suddenly her strange words were beginning to make sense to him. "You mean use the pain in my life...as a weapon?"

The little girl smiled. "If that is how you interpret it, then yes."

"But how?" Brad almost whined.

"The book is a tome of pain. Only those who have experienced pain in its purest form can truly decipher its meaning."

"Amy," Brad choked. "I lost my sister, who I loved dearly. Those things took her, and my father. I want revenge. I need it to complete me. Even if we get out of this mess, without it I would feel empty."

"Good," the little girl encouraged. "Good."

"But whose voice was that out there, who told me the page number to turn to?"

The little girl's smile suddenly vanished. "My father."

For just a second Brad forgot about the vampires in the hallway. His heart reached out to the little girl, feeling her loss and relating to it completely.

"Who was your father?"

The little girl smiled again. Her face brightened like a child on Christmas morning. "His name is Dr. Artimus Vinheiser. He is a prominent archeologist and a revered collector of ancient and historically important artifacts."

"I've heard of him before. I think I've seen him on TV before."

The little girl nodded. "He discovered the book while on one of his many expeditions to Northern Europe."

Her attention was suddenly diverted to the door. The top left corner of it was being bent inward, filling the room with a terrible noise. A single, pure white skeletal hand emerged from the opening, wavered in the air for a moment or two, clenched into a tight, angry fist. A thin trickle of bone-colored dust drifted down to the floor from it.

Brad turned around and bit his lip. The blood had drained from his face when he saw the clawed hand, a painting of impending death situated directly behind him, but he somehow pushed it out of his mind and focused on what the little girl was telling him.

"We have to hurry," he cried. "Tell me, what

did your father do?"

The little girl looked back into his eyes. "My father found the book and purchased it from a rare books dealer; he was anxious to add it to his collection, to uncover whatever secrets it held within its pages. He brought it home and started to delve into its mysteries, but was soon sidetracked by his other work. For months the book sat gathering dust and cobwebs, forgotten. It shared wall space with hundreds of other volumes, biding its time, and waiting." She looked over Brad's shoulder again at the door, a slight trace of fear etched on her face. "The book would not be denied, however, and eventually tapped into my father's mind to extract whatever pain it could."

Brad could hardly believe what he was hearing. He shook his head as if to rearrange the information. "The book extracted his pain?"

"It tried to, but found there was virtually none to take. Dr. Artimus Vinheiser had led a completely enviable life, void of pain or misfortune. His family always had wealth, and his health was robust."

The skeletal hand was soon joined by others. Within a few minutes there were at least ten of them, all thrashing back and forth, smashing into each other in vicious attempts to gain access to the room. Slimy black residue dripped down the grotesquely decorated surface of the door from several of the hands, coating it in a ghastly layer of stench and decay. The smell was becoming unbearable. He was suddenly glad his stomach was so empty.

He was sweating so much he could hardly keep his face dry. His head hurt and he felt his heart thumping wildly in his chest. The fact that he might not be able to take too much more weighed heavily on his weary and frightened mind. "Then what did the book do?" he asked, not really believing he was having this conversation or wanting to hear the answer.

The little girl sighed. "My father did have one great joy in his life. His work fulfilled him, but not completely. It nourished him, but only to the point that material accomplishments could. His wife was what really sustained him, kept him striving to be a better man, for her and for himself."

Brad found himself mesmerized by the little girl's words, but knew he did not have the luxury of listening to her complete story. Time was running out.

"Please, we have to hurry", he reminded her. "Those things are getting-"

The face peering at him through the small breach in the door froze his words in his mouth. The vampire stared at him with such hatred and evil that the expression alone was nearly enough to stop Brad's heart.

"And then it happened," the little girl added in a somber tone, oblivious to the malevolent creature glaring at them from the doorway. "The

31

day came like a lightening bolt, jarring my father loose from the comfort of his daily life, and sending him into deep despair."

"What happened?"

"His wife died and the book took advantage of his pain."

9

Questions swirled in Brad's mind like an insect swarm, but there, at the heart of them all, was one.

Why?

He reached for the core of his anger, found a memory.

"Brad, why don't ya go on an' help your little sister some. I don't feel like it right now," his father slurred. Brad could smell the whiskey on his breath and could see the irresponsible laziness in his bloodshot eyes. He would rather be drinking than taking care of his own daughter. "Go on, son, get going, ya hear me?" The words stung like a thousand needles.

Brad had learned to turn his anger with his father into a useful tool, a reminder to himself to be a better man, to try harder, to never give up. His father had stopped caring about anything when his wife had died, even his own children.

"Noooo!" Brad cried at the top of his lungs, releasing all the pent up rage and torment he had endured. The outburst was so sudden and salient that even the vampires paused in their assault on the door. After a few seconds they resumed their efforts, seemingly nourished by the anguish of their prey.

Brad struggled to maintain his composure. "I've tried my whole life to be strong, to never give up, but I feel like I'm nearing the end of my rope. I honestly don't know how much longer I can hold out."

The little girl smiled at him, wrapping him up in her warmth and confidence. "Use your pain. Defy the book as it tries to feed off of it."

Brad continued. "I've never had a true father figure, or a mother, either. I've always felt as if I was on my own. "

"Yes, continue. I understand."

"My life has been one thing after another, one problem leading into the next. My father was only a part of it, a big part granted, but still just a part of it." Brad noticed the book sitting on the desk behind him. There was a very faint greenish glow around it, which seemed to originate from beneath it, and spread out like cigarette smoke. It pulsed with movement, with some type of life. "I want this all to end! I'm sick of it! Sick of those filthy vampires, and sick of this stinking house!"

The book swelled, releasing a thick odor similar to rancid meat, but even more overpowering. It practically coated the room, leaving no corner untainted, staining everything with its corrupt stench.

The little girl noticed the book as well. Her eyes were fastened to it. Her thoughts racing with its movements. She knew what it was capable of, what it would do if it were able to.

"Now," she instructed Brad. "Twist your pain to your own will. Use it as a weapon, not a

34

deterrent to your goals and desires. The book will sense this and release its bonds on my father... hopefully."

Brad only partly understood what she was saying, but did as she said regardless. He flung his head back and gripped his painful memories and frustrations by the roots, swinging them around like a whip, twisting them to his desires, utilizing them to his own advantage. The memory of watching his father being yanked to his death by a vampire the size of a large gorilla, with a face to match, the only time Brad was actually glad that his father had drank himself into oblivion.

The memory of running to Mrs. Honner's house, seeking the solace and safety of her kindness.

Just as he arrived on her front porch her body was catapulted through the front bay window. Her head had been torn clean off and a short, half-decayed vampire squatted in her front room, munching on what was left of her face. The thing glared at him with such evil hunger and hatred that Brad's stomach expelled the remainder of his last meal onto the porch. The creature tossed her half-eaten head aside and bounded through the air straight for him, fangs gnashing, blood coating its stained and tattered shirt. The howl and throes of the creature after Brad impaled it with a spindle ripped from the porch frame. The fetid pile of pitch-black ash laced with an underlying putrid slime that marked the end of the vile monster.

And for the first time in his life, he actually felt like a true, red-blooded hero.

The vampires in the hallway wailed at the top of their dry-rotted lungs in frustration. Hundreds of the unnatural fiends howled and hissed, increasing their assault on the door. Above all the noise, on the other side of the door Brad heard Dr. Artimus Vinheiser. He was shouting and laughing cheers of relief, his jubilation rivaling the vampires' horrible screeching. Brad could hear him smashing against them, thrashing them within an inch of oblivion. Beating them to a powdery pulp. Doing what he could to end their terrible reign.

And then in a swift second, all was silent.

Both Brad and the little girl cautiously walked over to the door and pressed their ears to it, avoiding the trails of black ichor, holding their breath. The stillness was deafening and seemed to last for hours. Brad looked over at the little girl and smiled, and she smiled back at him. And then a single phrase filtered through the silence and into the room. It was simple, but its meaning was clear and powerful. The words cut through the hopelessness that had filled the library, offering promises of real hope that Brad had not felt in a long time.

"Thank you."

10

It had not been long since Brad had settled down to get some rest. The sleep he had managed to steal was troubled and sparse at best, but it was enough to sustain him and replenish his energy. He rubbed his swollen eyes and ran his fingers through his disheveled hair, noted it seemed to be thinning. Hunger and thirst competed for his attention, but he pushed them from his thoughts as best he could. They were the least of his worries.

"Hello. I hope you slept well enough. I was tempted to wake you, but thought better of it. You needed rest to regain your strength."

Brad sat up and stretched his aching limbs to the point of straining. "Good morning to you, too," he replied. His head felt like it had been run over by a truck, but overall he felt as if he would be able to get through the day. "How long was I out for?" he asked between yawns.

The little girl pushed the hair out of her face. "Approximately two hours, perhaps more."

"Boy, did I ever need that. Have there been any signs of those things?" Brad held on to a slight bit of hope that the vampires were gone, but resisted getting his hopes up too high. Experience had taught him to expect the worst.

"Absolutely nothing. Only the occasional squeaks and moans from an old house such as this one." Her expression did not reflect the ordeal she had been through. It was cheerful, full of promise and hope, and wholly unstained by recent events.

"Are you sure you're all right?" Brad asked. "I'm pretty sure I can find some first aid if you need any."

The little girl shook her head. "No, thank you," she politely replied. "I feel quite well."

Her attention quickly swung back to the door. Brad followed her eyes and realized that she must have been thinking of her father. He truly felt bad for her, but he remained reluctant to open the door. His instincts told him it still might be dangerous.

"I know you would like to see your father again," he said. "But until I'm a hundred percent sure it's safe out there I'm not going to open that door. Do you understand?"

The little girl looked up at him, her eyes watering. "I understand you perfectly," she answered. "I accepted a long time ago that my father would never return to me. I knew in my heart that I would never see his smile again, or hear his laugh, or feel his love. All these things I grew to acknowledge, despite the pain of doing so. But the mere thought 'the only barrier between him and I is that door' is almost too much to resist. I feel compelled to at least see if he is there, and if so, if he is all right."

Brad had a hard time arguing with her logic, especially since it was fairly obvious the vampires had gone. And sooner or later they would need to leave the room and find some food and water.

"Okay, fine," he finally conceded. "But I'm only opening it a few inches, just enough to see what's out there. Understand?" He hated to be so stern with her, especially after what they had been through, but at this point fear governed his actions, for better or worse.

The little girl nodded and promptly stood. She walked over to the door and rested her small hands on it. Brad watched her for a tense moment or two before walking up behind her and gently pushing her aside.

"All right then," he whispered nervously. "I hope we don't regret doing this."

"All will be well," the little girl replied with an innocent smile. "I know it will."

With effort tempered by reluctance Brad slid the heavy iron bar back and twisted the doorknob slightly. Fear laced his thoughts as he peered through the thin opening, squinting, hoping to God that there was nothing there.

The little girl hopped up and down behind Brad as she attempted to see through the opening. For the first time she was acting like a child her age. "Can you see anything?" she whispered anxiously. "Is there anyone there?"

Brad ignored her. His main concern was for their safety, not her curiosity or her desire to see her father.

"Take it easy," he said as he tried to look down the hallway through the thin crack in the doorway. "I'm trying to see if there's anyone there."

He scanned back and forth as best as he could, but the lighting in the hallway was not very good. Only sporadic beams of pale moonlight filtered into the passage, sporadically illuminating empty corners and sparse, dusty walls loosely decorated with forgotten relics and pictures. The floor revealed only traces of the creatures' remains; a few distorted footprints scattered about in sooty black residual ash, and some rotted pieces of cloth that seemed very old, somehow perverse in design.

Brad exhaled deeply as he felt a world of worry slide off his shoulders. For the first time in ages he felt as if there might actually be hope for the future of mankind, and for himself. He had been at war with his own guilt for as long as he had with the vampires.

The little girl was practically jumping up

and down. "Is my father there? Is my father there?" she continually asked. "Do you see him? Is he there?"

Brad hated to disappoint her. "I'm sorry honey," he solemnly said. "But I don't see anything except for some ashes and a few pieces of old clothing. Your father must have succeeded. I think he destroyed them."

Against his better judgment Brad began to open the door a little more. He was very cautious, but still felt vulnerable. The realization that he needed some type of weapon struck him suddenly, and he looked back into the room to see if there was anything he could use.

He quickly walked over to the desk and tore off a piece of wood from one of the drawers. It was crude, but sharp, and would probably be effective if he needed it.

The book sat on the edge of the desk, its power undiminished. Brad felt it tap into his thoughts, compelling him to open it, to delve into its terrible secrets once again.

Brad felt the evil pull from the book, but pushed it aside fairly easily. Strange and perverse as its influence was, he had locked down his emotions the night Amy died. He would make sure that he was the one in control. With a quick jab he pushed the book off the edge of the desk, causing it to land with a heavy thud on the dusty floor. It sunk almost an inch as soon as it landed, leaving a deep impression in the metal as small dust clouds settled back on the floor.

Brad swung back around and strutted toward the open doorway where the little girl stood waiting for him. "Follow me," he instructed. "And above all, stay close."

12

The hallway loomed before them like a cold, dark tunnel. It radiated a strange type of aura, similar to a long forgotten prison, deserted but still powerful in its desolation, still haunted by the evil deeds of its former occupants. Brad was sure he still heard faint echoes of the creaking and screeching the deformed door had made as he had slowly pushed it open, as if they were in a deep cavern instead of a house.

"Stay close," Brad reminded the little girl. "We don't know anything for sure. Just because it looks safe doesn't mean it is." His mind flashed back to Mrs. Honner's brutal demise.

The little girl clung to his shirt. She held on both out of fear and from her desire to follow his instructions. She knew that even if she found her father he probably would not, or could not, help them much, if at all. In a lot of ways they were on their own.

"I will," she promised with a small nod, and positioned herself as close to Brad as she could.

Thin rays of moonlight streamed into the hallway from three small overhead skylights, mainly, but only slightly, due to the increasing cloud cover outside. It seemed as if the corridor was a mile long with no promise of safety or security at the end of it. All it offered was a path.

The first few steps into the hallway were some of the most difficult Brad had ever taken in his life. He felt as if he were a toddler who was just learning to walk, stumbling and ready to latch onto any nearby table or chair for support. Only this time his life was at stake.

"Stay close to me," he repeated, more for himself than for the little girl. "No matter what happens, stay close." His experiences had him entertaining the horrible, but very real, possibility of something happening to her. Just the thought of it sent an ice-cold shiver down his spine. He vowed to himself that he would die before he let anything happen to the nameless little girl.

They carefully moved forward, waiting a few seconds between each step to make sure there were no consequences. Dangers could be lurking around every corner, within every shadow, inside every unseen area. There was no real way to be sure except to move forward, survey the situation and move forward again. However, they might not have much time, so being overly cautious was not a luxury they could really afford, either.

Brad picked up his pace slightly and the little girl followed close behind him. The vampires could attack at any moment, a fact not lost on him, and he felt that getting out of the house might be their best chance for survival. What had once promised a sanctuary now felt like a prison. *Or worse.*

"Let me know if you see any signs of my father," the little girl whispered. "Please, I need to know whether he is still alive."

"Don't worry honey," Brad replied without taking his eyes off his surroundings. "I'll let you know."

The little girl smiled nervously. "Thank you very much. I mean it."

Brad smiled as well but still kept his eyes on the hallway ahead of them. "Don't mention it," he said. "Don't mention it at all."

The sound was small at first, escalating gradually until it reached a level impossible to ignore. It faintly resembled sharp nails gliding across a chalkboard, but far more unnerving. Apparently, something was trying to get into the house.

Brad froze where he stood, the little girl bumped into him.

"What is that sound?" she asked breathlessly. "Where is it coming from?"

Brad's eyes narrowed. "I'm not sure, but I think it's from around the corner, possibly near the front doorway. We'll have to pass by there if we want to get out of here. I don't think there's any way of avoiding it."

He tried to suppress a thought that fluttered into his weary mind, but failed and it took root there. *What if whatever's outside the house making those noises is not trying to get in, at least not yet, anyway? Suppose it's trying to gain access, not to the house, but to my mind?*

Toying with its prey in a demented game of cat and mouse. Brad shuddered, chided himself for letting his imagination go there, but continued to creep forward.

The hallway ended approximately fifteen feet ahead, where it branched off to the left, which led directly to the front door, and to the right, which led to one of the main living rooms. A huge crystal chandelier hung over the front foyer and another near the entranceway to the living room. Neither of them provided any light. The only illumination was from thin beams of faint moonlight cascading in through the cracks in the front door frame.

Brad flicked the light switches as he came across them, but they yielded only empty clicks.

"There's no power in the whole house," he moaned in dismay. "Those filthy things must have torn down the lines or something." *Or they've destroyed the power station.* He took a deep breath and tried to steady his frayed nerves. "We'll have to try to find some candles or a flashlight."

The little girl nodded and continued staring ahead. The noises were subsiding a little.

"I don't think we'll be able to make it out the front door," Brad whispered. "Whatever is making those noises... the sound seems to be coming from there, more or less. It might be right outside the house waiting for us. I think we'll stand a better chance if we try to go through the house, even find another way out besides the back door." He watched her expression to see if she disagreed, if she had anything to add.

The little girl nodded in agreement and gripped Brad's hand tightly. "If you say so," she whispered. "But I'm not exactly sure of the best way to go. Most of the time I have lived here my father was hesitant to leave too many lights on. He said it hurt his eyes and clouded his judgment. This house has always stood in shadows. Always. Like shadows are part of this building."

"You mean to tell me you have no idea how this place is laid out, or where the back door is?" Brad tried to control his irritation, but his grip on his temper was wearing thin again.

The little girl nodded. "I'm afraid not."

Brad clenched his jaw and pulled her along behind him. "Fine, then, I'll just have to find a way out of this place on my own."

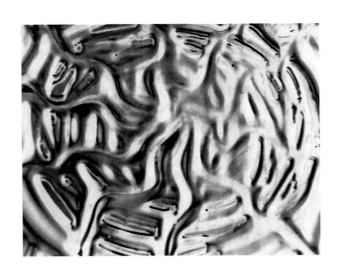

13

Every step Brad and the little girl took felt like a mile. Shadows hung in every corner like jet-black lions waiting to pounce on prey. He felt as if they were going around in circles. The house was in some way distorted, unnatural in its design. Walls came out of nowhere and met at tilted angles, impossibly holding up heavy ceilings and fixtures. Dark shadows sprawled across large areas unbroken. Floors sunk toward one side, but met with neighboring walls at higher spots, defying the laws of physics and common sense.

Brad rubbed his aching head and swollen eyes. He felt as if they were in a funhouse, although this place was far more sinister. Vampires could still be lurking inside it, and a heavy sense of dread hung in the stagnant air, choking whatever hope remained.

His mind touched on memories of the neighborhood carnivals of his childhood. The aura surrounding all of the rides and booths was both frightening and intoxicating. But back then he was able to rely on his youth and exuberance to overcome all the unsettling aspects associated with carnivals and their workforce. And most important of all, he was able to go home afterward, and leave the weirdness behind. This dark funhouse offered no such securities or promises. There were no safe places anymore, and he was certain now that this house was farther from safe than most.

"I think the kitchen area is through that way," the little girl whispered, pointing toward another long hallway. "I can't be entirely sure, though."

Brad looked down at her. He did not want to trust their lives to a strange child who did not know her way around her own home, but was desperate enough to consider it. He was beginning to doubt his own judgment, and the possibility that the little girl just might be right prompted him to follow her suggestion.

"All right," he said hesitantly. "If you feel that is the way to go, we'll try it. I guess as long as we're heading away from those noises...." A light smile creased his face, and he looked at her to try reassure them both. *I hope you're right, though.*

The corridor led from the cavernous family room down into another long, strangely designed passage. It, too, felt unnatural, almost to the point of being cartoonish, as if rendered in an animated setting. Brad hesitated before walking down the hallway, clenching the piece of wood from the desk so tightly his hand ached.

The walls, in keeping with the general theme of the rest of the house, were adorned with more antiquities. Brad wished Dr. Vinheiser had decorated with a lighter, more cheerful theme. *Anything would have been better than "ancient creepy."*

"Stay close," Brad reminded the little girl. "Remember, we're still not sure where we are going in this crazy place."

The little girl nodded. "It is odd," she tilted her head and noted with her gaze a couple of the walls. Her voice remained calm and steady, "My memory of this house is vague at best, but I do not recall the strange architectural designs here before."

Brad immediately froze. "What do you mean?"

"I am not sure this house was constructed this way. Perhaps the situation has altered it somehow."

Brad felt his empty stomach churn. He believed he had seen all the horror the world had to offer: Vampires, loved ones killed literally right before his eyes, strange little girls who seemed to be from another world. But now, houses which had been altered into some weird mockery of common sense? It pushed on his mind that such a thing might be possible, but more so that his strange little hostess could propose such a possibility.

She doesn't even know her own name, or where her kitchen is. And I'm looking to her for help.

His hope for escape from the house withered. He felt insanity tapping on the walls of his mind, trying to gain entry into his psyche.

54

14

Dr. Artimus Vinheiser stumbled through the room, unsure of where he was or how he had gotten there. The dim glow from the moonlight streaming through several small skylights strained his eyes and caused his head to ache, but he pressed on. Fearing the worst, the price of his past deeds weighed heavily on his soul as well as his body. Bruises covered his torso and arms and blood trickled from numerous lacerations across his exhausted body. All he wanted to do was find his daughter; she was the only thing that mattered now. He knew, felt, she was nearby. And even now, especially now, he trusted his instincts without question.

Horrible memories roamed across his weary mind. Thoughts of the birth of his daughter and the corrupt temptations he had succumbed to thereafter. He had meant well, he constantly reminded himself, but history would not be so kind in its evaluation of him, of that he was certain. *Assuming there would be anyone left to read about it.*

The walls seemed to impede his every step, lashing out in inanimate attempts to thwart his progress. The ceiling dangled overhead, swaying back and forth as if in a twisted dream, threatening to crash down on his head at any moment. He pushed on, energized by his desire to find his only child and fulfill his destiny.

His blurred vision made it difficult to focus on what lay before him, but he was just able to see the outline of where he was. He knew the house well, at least he had before it started to warp, and even though the stench of the fiends still lingered in its darkened rooms, his mind was clear enough to navigate through it. With some help he had managed to destroy the vampires who had forced their way into the house, but he was still unsure of just how many remained outside. Hundreds, he feared, perhaps more.

He did not see the large painting as it materialized out of thin air, manifesting directly in front of his face. He smashed into it head first and crashed to the ground. Lying on his back, trying to focus on the illusive ceiling through dust clogging his senses, the heavy brass-framed painting fell on top of him. It covered his body almost completely, from head to toe, like a blanket, molding itself to the contours of his body.

His weary bloodshot eyes finally focused on the face of death painted on the enormous canvas looming just in front of his nose, threatening to suffocate him. He saw the swirling chaos of black and purple skies and twisting storms entwining the fearsome landscape with jagged bolts of razor-sharp lightening. He saw snarled gaping maws sprouting up out of the rugged ground, sporting infinite rows of gnashing bloodied teeth, grinding up and down as if chewing invisible bodies to gory pulps. He saw the house in the background, his house, the house he was now trapped inside, and he saw himself near the front porch of that same house, bent over at impossible angles, a caricature of his former self, a twisted imitation of his humanity. He was straddling something, someone, at his feet, leering with an expression of hate-filled hunger and power-mad domination. He was towering over the prone figure as if he were master, judge and jury. Even god.

Dr. Vinheiser closed his eyes and welcomed unconsciousness, allowed himself to fall into the welcome darkness of sleep. On some level he felt it might be his only alternative, his only escape from the nightmare that plagued his every waking moment. And he knew he would see his daughter again in his dreams.

15

Brad heard the noise from the other side of the house, as did the little girl. They looked at each other with expressions of worry and hope. Maybe there was another person in the house, someone who needed help, or could help them find a way out.

"We should follow the noise. Maybe it leads to a way out." Brad feared that it was another vampire, but something inside his mind assured him it was not.

They started to make their way toward the sound of the crash. The darkness still obstructed their path and they had to feel their way along more than ever. The walls felt cold and damp, the drywall sinking in slightly with every touch of their hands, crumbling beneath the soggy wallpaper. Brad and the little girl continued to move forward, unsure of where exactly they were going. They knew very well that they could not turn back.

"Can you see anything yet?" the little girl asked quietly.

"No, nothing yet," Brad replied.

He found himself wondering about the book back in the library. Was it really as powerful as she had said? And did it still pose a threat to them? He was not sure, but forced himself to block out any thoughts of it and focus on navigating through the house that seemed to be rotting, or melting, around them. At least the floor seemed solid enough, though it had become more uneven as they made their way to the elusive kitchen.

When Brad and the little girl reached the room from which they were sure the noise had come, they found a large space, dominated by ancient-looking relics and various odds and ends, the sort of stuff a collector would display. And laying in the opposite doorway was an enormous painting, which seemed to be covering something lumpy and roughly the size of a person. Both were completely still.

They bolted over to the painting. Brad quickly pulled the heavy painting aside, and cleared loose debris from a man's face. He was an aged man, possibly in his seventies, and sported a thin white-gray mustache and neatly-trimmed pointed beard. His face was lined with wrinkles and bore the weathering of many years of exploration. But he was nonetheless a handsome man, whose broad build and tasteful attire attested to good breeding and education. It appeared he was a gentleman who took care of himself.

"Is this your father?" Brad asked the little girl.

She knelt at the injured man's side and grasped his hand in hers. "Yes," she whispered. "He is my father."

Artimus Vinheiser opened his eyes and gazed into the face of his daughter.

Despite his condition he recognized her

instantly, a slight, painful smile creasing his weathered face.

"I recognize you my child," he said softly. "You have no idea just how long I have been searching for you." He began to cough uncontrollably, but regained his composure as best he could. "I never thought I would see you again."

"You've been looking for her?" Brad asked incredulously. "I thought you left her here, in this house. I...I thought...."

Dr. Vinheiser shook his head slightly, groaned from the discomfort. The heavy canvas had succeeded in compounding his injuries, which were already critical. "No, sir, I did not leave her in this wretched house, at least not by my own choice. I was separated from her by force, a force far greater than any other on this weary planet. A force capable of evil and power beyond the scope of any mere mortal. Something which I could not control, nor even resist."

Brad's look of concern and confusion instantly vanished and was replaced by one of resignation and fear. "The book. It's the book isn't it?"

"Yes, it is the book. *The Tome of Pain*, as it is known in its own plane, in its own world."

The little girl was fighting back tears. Her tangled loose hair hung in front of her dirty face, and her tiny hands shook uncontrollably. It had been so long since she had seen her father;

she did not know what to say. All she could do was simply hold his hand and listen to him.

"The book created pain within my life and nourished itself from it," Dr. Vinheiser continued. "It enveloped my soul within its pages, draining whatever happiness there was, growing stronger as it did so."

"But couldn't you have realized what it was and try and stop it, or throw it away, or burn it, anything?"

Dr. Vinheiser sighed. "Can an alcoholic put down the bottle? Can a drug addict throw away the needle? You don't understand and probably never will, but the book had a hold on my will far beyond any control I still possessed. I could destroy it no more than a mother could her own child."

Brad had heard enough. He abruptly stood up and brushed himself off. "For your information sir," he retorted. "I have been acquainted more or less with the book. Just ask your own daughter here." He motioned towards the little girl. "She saw me defeat the book. She saw me manage to overcome it. What do you think destroyed those vampires outside your library? I did. And I am not a particularly strong person. But I still did it. If I could do it, you could have, too."

Instantly Brad felt a pang of guilt and regret for raising his voice like he did, especially in front of the little girl, but did not apologize. All he wanted to do was find a way out of the

62

house. If he could help the little girl as well, then so much the better, but she had her father with her now, and she was no longer his responsibility.

"We need to get out of here now," he announced. "How do we find the back door out of this place?"

Dr. Vinhesier laughed, coughing up droplets of blood in the process. "My dear boy," he croaked. "There isn't a rear door anymore. The house is being twisted by the book to prevent us from leaving. It is probably still hungry and needs to feed again." He weakly lifted his hand and loosened his collar. "I'm sure you have noticed that things around here lately have been a little, shall we say, distorted. It's the book, bending things to its own desires, weaving another truth, another reality, one where those unnatural creatures and desolation rule the Earth. It searched for suitable carriers of its evil, and it eventually found them."

Brad's control of himself slipped some. He was tired of the Vinheisers, tired of the book and this twisted house, tired of all their nonsense. "Listen, I just want to get out of this crazy place. I want no part of demonic books or vampires or little girls and their long lost fathers." Brad breathed, as deeply as his constricted chest would allow, and continued through clenched teeth, "I just want out of here and the best way to do that is to find the back door."

The little girl looked up at Brad with watery eyes.

"I'm sorry that I said that," Brad apologized to her. "But I've managed to get through an awful lot by myself, and I think we'd all be better off on our own from now on." He felt his temper running away with him, but saw no reason to rein it in.

"And what then? What will you do after you've escaped from this house? Surely you are aware that there are many more of those creatures roaming about, possibly right outside the doors of this very building. You must realize that wherever you go, no matter how far away from here it is, that you will never be able to escape from the vampires, or the book, or worse, from yourself." Dr. Vinheiser's voice became strained, and another wave of pain nearly overtook him.

"What is that supposed to mean?" Brad cried. "And how do you know about all this?" He raised an eyebrow at the injured man.

Dr. Vinheiser closed his eyes and forced himself to sit up slightly. He had several broken ribs, and bruises over most of his body, but still managed to suppress his discomfort enough to look Brad in the eyes. "Unfortunately, I'm afraid I had something to do with it."

16

The night air was growing cooler. Thin plumes of gray mist gently wrapped around every leafless tree limb and bush. Off in the distance a lone coyote howled to the pale, full moon, raising its conical snout high above the cold, barren ground as it spewed its night-song into the wastelands.

The vampires crouched low to the once-fertile ground. Their numbers had increased many times over, allowing them to disperse themselves into legions capable of overpowering small villages, or even cities. The larger and more aggressive of their kind led the smaller, less dominant ones by sheer brute force and cruelty. Cannibalism was not uncommon within their ranks, and what one did, the others more or less followed without question.

An enormous, seven-and-a-half foot tall vampire scowled when it caught sight of the large house looming far in the distance. Gifted with excellent eyesight, it could see for miles. It sensed the beings within the building were humans, possibly many of them, and it also sensed something else there as well. Its cold, clammy hands clenched in anger, a jet-black drop of ichor trickled down to the soil. It raised its sinewy arms high into the night sky and wailed as loud as it could. Throngs of scampering creatures quickly crowded around the large fiend, blotting out the moon hanging low in the sky, trampling any residual plant life underfoot. They gazed at each other with heated expressions and dripping fangs. They would join the others near the house in the distance very soon. Apparently they had also sensed something in the house, since they constantly scurried around the building.

The large fiend wondered why they had not overtaken the prey within already. Even now the earlier arrivals were not trying to break into the house. It watched them merely scuttle back and forth around the perimeter of the building, tapping and scratching with their claws on various sections, moaning to the night sky, growling at each other.

The large fiend swung its baleful gaze back towards the coyote in the distance, still howling to the rising full moon, but decided not to pursue the scrawny animal, despite the deep need to kill any living creature it found. Something in the house promised far more than a morsel of meat.

It growled and grunted and pushed its way to the fore edge of the horde. With unearthly speed and agility the mass of vampires rushed toward the house, over the small hills and dead grass, led by the largest, most ferocious fiend of them all.

17

Brad walked away from Dr. Vinhesier and the little girl. His conscience weighed heavily on his mind, but he still did not stop to look back at them or reconsider, content that he was doing the right thing. He was confident being on his own was the only reason he had managed to stay alive as long as he had.

"Wait," the little girl pleaded.

Despite himself, Brad stopped in his tracks.

"Please, if you must go, then at least take this with you, it could save your life." She reached into her inside pocket and withdrew the same odd-looking device that Brad had used in the library to unlock the mechanism on the book. Its thin arms jutted out from its sides as if ready to clamp down onto the book again.

Brad slowly retraced his steps until he was close enough, reached for the odd key and carefully took it from her.

"What do I need this for?" he asked.

The little girl smiled at him through her tangled hair. "You should hold onto it for now. I would recommend that you retrieve the book as well. Keep them together, keep them apart, but do not allow them to vanish under the moon."

More riddles. Brad certainly did not want to take that terrible book with him, but for some reason he trusted the little girl. He tucked the device into his pocket and slowly began to creep toward the library to get the book. And as he walked away he looked back at the father and daughter he was leaving behind. The love the two of them shared was obvious, and it painfully reminded him of the family that he had lost.

But it also reminded him that even in a world as messed up as this one right now, there were still some things that mattered. There was something even more powerful than vampires or demonic books bent on world domination.

Love.

He turned around again and called out to Dr. Vinheiser and the little girl. "We can make it out of this place if we stick together," he announced. "Come on now, let's get a move on. There's probably not much time left before those things figure out a way in here."

"No," the little girl said somberly. "We cannot go with you. Our place is here, within this house, at this moment in time. Our being together, my father and I, will save us all. We can't expect you to understand, but you must have faith."

Well, it's good to know she understands that I don't understand. But he could not refuse himself the question: "Why on Earth would you want to stay in this place?"

Dr. Vinheiser pushed himself upright as much as he could. "She speaks the truth. We don't expect you to fully understand, in fact I didn't expect her to understand it yet either, but it is now clear to me that she does so, completely."

Brad accepted there was no way he could talk them out of staying behind. Acceptance without understanding had become a familiar feeling to him. It still felt like giving up, each and every time, but he was weary, and could expend no more energy on the incomprehensible pair.

"All right, then," Brad quietly replied. "I respect your wishes, although I do wish you two would leave with me now."

"Good luck," Dr. Vinhesier responded with a smile. "I have strong faith in your abilities, and know that you will make it."

"Thank you sir," Brad said with an equally bright smile.

Brad turned and walked away again, leaving the little girl and her father behind, oblivious to the absolute absurdity of his sudden change in mood. He was reciting a prayer for them under his breath, hoping to God that they would be all right, but he had to focus on another important matter as well. Getting out of the house alive.

18

Vampires were collecting in vast numbers around the house, led by the brutally despotic new leader. The others followed its instructions, mainly out of fear. With swift and flawless calculations the vampire leader determined precisely where in the house the humans were located. Every possible escape route from the building was covered completely.

It stood back and watched the others circling the house. Confident in its strategy, it only waited for the right time to strike. The other object he sensed in the house was shielded from its inner vision just enough so it could not completely make out what or where the mysterious prize was.

It was something of great power, and for this reason alone the big brute desired its possession, but it also troubled the fiend to some extent. Why was this object, of all things on this forsaken planet, hidden from perception?

It licked jagged fangs in anticipation, slicing its oily tongue in the process. *So hungry*, as were they all, but patience had gotten them this far, and there was insufficient reason to abandon it now. Until it could determine more about the bigger prize inside the house, and make sure it was not some bait in a clever trap, it would continue to monitor the house and it contained.

Just a little longer.

19

Brad heard the noises outside the house. The almost gentle scratching of curved talons across the sides of the home was threatening his sanity. But he suspected that was exactly what the vampires were trying to do. If they could cause him to lose control, and possibly jeopardize the lives of the little girl and her father, then they could feed on their minds as well as their bodies.

He was finding it very difficult to locate the library, even though he knew where it was, or had been, or should be. The hallways had grown even longer, stretching far beyond the boundaries of common sense. Walls swayed back and forth as if alive, paintings and pictures distorted into grotesque mockeries of their former grandeur, fixtures flickered on and off, creating a surreal landscape of madness. Brad was too focused on finding his way to wonder where the power was coming from.

A faint greenish smog hung heavily in the air, clogging Brad's nose and stinging his eyes. It was very similar to the stench that the book had emitted in the library. It obstructed his view of what laid before him, yet another of the house's attempt to block his path. *Accepting that now, are you?* he asked himself, but Brad pushed on, motivated by the memory of the little girl and her dying father, and eventually he found the library.

When he pushed the heavy door open at first he did not see the book. The desk sat where it was before, but there was nothing on it, nor on the floor near it. Brad clearly remembered the indentation the book had made when it hit the floor, yet there was no trace of it nearby. Only by searching on his hands and knees did he find the book lying in a far corner of the room underneath several similarly sized volumes. Brad entertained the notion that the book was hiding from him, concealing itself as best it could. He grabbed it, and ignoring the revulsion he felt at the contact, tucked it under his arm and sprinted back out of the room.

The corridors of the house bent and twisted, causing Brad to bang into walls and knock down paintings and pictures. The mist was becoming thicker, disorienting him and draining his energy and will. It invaded every pore in his body, every thought in his mind.

Is it the house? Or perhaps the book? Or maybe they were in conjunction with one another, working in harmony to eliminate the humans who were trying to escape.

Brad found himself stumbling towards the front door. He wanted to turn around and go the other way, but Dr. Vinheiser's words about there not being a rear door anymore resonated in his clouded mind.

But what about the attic? What if he could find a way up into the attic of the house? At least from there he could possibly see outside, perhaps through an air vent or window, and see exactly what the situation outside was, if there were indeed any more vampires roaming about, and if so, how many and where they were.

Despair crept into his planning, and told him even if he could find a way into the attic, which in itself would be difficult and no doubt dangerous, there would be no guarantee that he could even see anything outside. And how would he ever be able to escape the house? Being trapped in a confined space such as an attic was not a wise option.

With great reluctance Brad resigned himself that his only logical way out of the house was through the front door. He clutched the book to his chest, and hoping it would somehow offer protection of some sort, gripped the splintered chunk of wood he still clutched like a talisman, and slowly walked toward the door.

The scratching noises had diminished to a light scraping here and there. They were still frighteningly deliberate, but were less threatening somehow. Brad thinly hoped that the monsters were disbanding, but reminded himself it was better to be prepared for the worst.

20

Dr. Vinheiser was slipping in and out of consciousness as the little girl cradled his head in her lap, caressing his face and looking into his eyes.

"Father," she whispered. "I am afraid I do not fully understand what my role is going to be. I know only that I am destined to save humanity, and offer myself, my love, for its survival."

Dr. Vinheiser opened his weary eyes and looked at his tiny daughter. He knew very well what must be done, however much it pained his heart and soul. His love was insignificant compared to the importance of the task he must complete.

"I know my child," he moaned softly. "I know. We must be strong, *you* must be strong. Have faith in not only our destinies, but also in our everlasting souls. There is more than this, I am sure of it." He passed out then, eliciting a worried and mournful groan from the little girl.

"Father! Father! Don't leave me. Not now!"

Dr. Vinheiser was roused slightly by her plea, but did not open his eyes. "I am still here child. Fear not. The abominations outside the house must be let in. You must find your way to the front door of the house and release the locks. Hurry now, there is not much time left before the house itself will be directed by the book to destroy us all, and with us, humanity."

The little girl understood. "I love you father," she said through a strained smile.

"And I you, my sweet child. Now go. Hurry along, I say."

Dr. Vinheiser listened as his tiny daughter scuttled away from him down the hallway. The pain and loneliness that gripped his soul felt cold, but he endured it for the sake of the world. It was the right thing to do. And now all he could do was wait.

21

The lead vampire bristled with excitement. The change it had detected within the house fueled its hunger. The object was close at hand, very close to where it stood. Soon the prize, and anything else the creature desired, would be for the taking. It reveled in the anticipation that after it had the object in its talons it would be powerful enough to reign over all in this world.

The other vampires jostled back and forth near the front door. Their leader had instructed them to suppress their assaults on the house. They sensed that soon they would gain access to the building and anything inside of it.

22

Brad hesitated at the front door. The three locking mechanisms were within easy reach, yet he did not touch them. Something was holding him back, despite his desperation to escape the house. A cold, impossible breeze from nowhere drifted into his face. Should he unlock the door? Or should he merely play it safe and wait to see if the vampires had completely gone? The book he held was growing heavier with each passing second, and he sensed soon he would no longer be able to carry it.

Brad winced as painful memories crept into his head, rooted to his fear and refusing to relinquish their hold on his mind. It was like being an unwilling audience to a horror film in which he was dashing from one gory scene to the next. Amy was dead. His father was dead. Mrs. Honner was dead. And there was a good chance that everyone he knew was dead.

He fought back the urge to cry, afraid doing so would make him somehow less of a man. An ideal gifted to him by his father. Brad had been able to uphold that ideal his whole life so far, but he knew he was failing now. *There's no point in escaping the house, the old man was right, there's no escape from them.* His head hung heavily and he sobbed.

And then he heard her.

The little girl was running toward him. Her

face was a frenzied mixture of relief and sorrow. She knew what she had to do, but was obviously distraught over it.

"Brad!" she cried out to him. "Please, you must not touch the door. You must stay where you are!"

"Don't worry, I'm not going anywhere." The strength had drained from his legs, they felt like rubber, and his head throbbed from hunger and exhaustion. He still held the book, but was ready to drop it. It simply hurt too much to hold on. It felt like it was sliding itself into his mind, latching onto his thoughts, corrupting his humanity.

The house twisted and churned. Walls wavered back and forth, taking on a watery consistency. Everywhere, swirling plumes of fiery gas erupted from the floor, which itself gyrated as if alive. Deep chasms opened up in every room revealing darkness unmatched in its depth and promise of despair.

The little girl was doing her best to make it through the house. She kept her eyes on Brad, and frequently reminded him to stay put and not let go of the book until she reached him.

The floor in front of her opened up into a pitch-black gulf, and the little girl doubled her efforts to reach where Brad sat, helpless. She leapt over the hole, barely landed on the other side and twisted her ankle. She crashed to the floor in pain, but still yelled for Brad to remain where he was.

23

Outside the front door vampires were beginning to mill around with greater urgency. They occasionally fought with each other, but under the watchful eye of their leader, they remained somewhat orderly.

"Remain still!" the leader growled. "The prey are loose within the house, as is the object. We will soon have both."

Another large fiend, nearly as big as the leader, grumbled heavily, its foul breath causing even the other vampires to shrink back in disgust.

"We should attack immediately," it snarled, blood-red eyes glaring with hatred. "We are wasting time strolling around here like foolish cattle. There is food inside, only separated from us by flimsy walls and glass. We must act now!"

"Silence!" the leader commanded. "The object within is far more important than another paltry meal."

The other vampires, fearing the wrath of their leader, glared at the outspoken one. By the sheer weight of their numbers they silenced it forever, nourishing themselves on its deformed body and twisted mind.

24

Dr. Vinheiser's eyes rolled back in his head; he was having trouble staying awake. His injuries were fatal, but he had to stay alert as long as he could. He had to make sure that his daughter made it to the front door of the house. He had to make sure she would let the vampires in.

The little girl crawled across the shifting floors, slowly making her way to Brad, who sat on the treacherous floor, the book clutched fast to his body, his head hanging over it in despair. Time was running out. Soon the vampires would release their pent up rage and power and assault the house right down to its very foundation, utterly destroying all those within and humanity's last chance at survival.

Brad's mind was losing the battle with the book. The *Tome* was conquering his will, inducing his mind to disbelieve any of this was happening.

"It's all right," he happily chanted over and over again. "No real problems here, just make-believe ones. We'll be just fine. Just fine."

The little girl crawled as fast as she could across the buckling floor. The house hindered her at every opportunity, slid furniture toward her, dropped drywall down on her from above. "Hang on Brad," she cried. "I'm almost there."

Brad just hummed to himself as if he were all alone. His mind was only occupied with pleasant thoughts. Memories of his father in happier times, of Amy strolling down the sidewalk, her hair flowing around her pretty face. What the world had been like before.

The vampire leader finally abandoned patience when it sensed the object in the house was very near to the front door. The book was calling out to it, sending out a beacon that it was on the other side of the door. Compelled to action, he ordered the others to attack.

They began to thrash violently against the front door. It was made of wrought iron, nearly four inches thick, but they did not care. They, too, sensed the presence of a strange and powerful object within the house, and their lust for blood and power would not be denied. With great, unyielding blows they relentlessly assaulted the last barrier in their way.

The little girl heard the vampires outside the door, and she re-doubled her efforts to reach Brad before it was too late.

"I'm coming. I'm coming," she cried. "Please don't move. And whatever you do, don't open the door!"

Brad barely heard her. He was becoming lost within the lies of the book.

His mind swayed back and forth, between reality and insanity, between the false utopia the book offered and the real danger he was in. He no longer knew the difference, or cared for that matter. More and more his only concern was holding onto the book, making sure it was safe from harm, doing what it told him to do. He cradled it in his arms, caressing it lovingly. He hardly felt the thin, curved talon slice into the back of his neck. One of the vampires had breached the front door, and managed to slip one of its claws through the opening.

Warm, rich blood dripped down Brad's back, soaking his tattered shirt and pooling on the floor. The vampires smelled the blood and increased their assault on the door. Heavy crashes echoed throughout the house as the fiends relentlessly tried to get at their prey. Slate-gray hands tipped with two-inch, dirt-encrusted claws reached around every corner of the door, swatting at the air in vain attempts to grab anything within reach.

Just as the leader's huge claw ripped clean through the door and reached for Brad's throat, the little girl fell across his lap and tore the book from his hands.

25

"It's all right now," the little girl whispered into Brad's ear. "Everything will be all right now."

Brad's vision was blurred and he had trouble making out exactly who, or what, was standing above him. His back ached and his legs were so cramped he could hardly move, but his memory, his mind, was gradually coming back to him, and with them his free will.

"W...what's going on?" he mumbled. "Where am I?"

The little girl smiled down at him and helped him to his feet. "We're still in my father's house, near the front door."

Brad stood up, brushed himself off, felt the bloody wound on his neck. The pain was dull, but still enough to warrant his attention. He ripped off a piece of his shirt and wrapped it around the wound.

"What happened to those things that were trying to get inside? Where are they?"

The polluted breath on the back of his neck stung his wound and drove fear straight into his soul. Too afraid to turn around he merely stood where he was and waited for the inevitable response to his questions.

"Yes, foolish one," the raspy voice slurred. "We are here."

They speak English? Brad stared at the little girl. She was still standing in front of him, oddly she was still smiling. The thought that somehow she, too, could be connected with the vampires occurred to Brad, but he pushed it aside. Her own father lay in another part of the house dying. Surely the little girl had not forgotten about him.

Brad decided if he was going to die, then he at least wanted to understand why.

"What is going on here?" he demanded to know. "Are you a part of this?" he asked the little girl.

The little girl merely looked deep into his eyes and tilted her head. She did not speak, nor make any attempt to escape. And something inside of Brad told him that she had as little to do with the invasion as he did.

The vampires were collecting inside of the house, filling the rooms with their grotesque bodies and evil intentions. The leader moved forward and wrapped its long arms around Brad in an iron grip. Brad could not move a muscle or even cry out in pain. He was as helpless as a newborn baby. Just when he was about to pass out, the fiend suddenly dropped him to the floor.

"Little one," it drawled. "Before my minions and I take pleasure in your pain and death you shall willingly hand over the object you are so obviously hiding behind your puny back." The creature's long sinewy arms flailed high above its deformed head, smacked into the ceiling.

Why doesn't it just take the book from her? Brad wondered.

"Give me the object now!" the leader commanded with even more authority than before. "Do as I say!"

Brad could see the thing clenching its fists in rage. Finally, it calmed and crossed its arms, observing the little girl as it did so.

"I see. We'll just have to feed first. There will be time after the feast for the other."

Swiftly it gestured for the multiplying vampires who were filing into the house to line up in an organized fashion. They obeyed without question, only mumbling animalistic grunts.

Brad watched helplessly as the monsters scooped up the little girl and threw her into the far corner of the room. She smacked hard into the wall, but still managed to hold onto the book.

She looked up at Brad, her battered face covered in blood. "Everything will be all right," she repeated to him. "Everything will be all right."

Slowly, the vampires advanced, savouring their victory. Brad managed to stand up only to be knocked back across the room by a particularly short, stocky vampire. It gloated screeched with joy at its successful assault.

When Brad came to, he felt cold breath that smelled like an open grave on his face. There were at least a dozen hideous expressions inches away from him, studying him, sizing him up.

"Well, what are you waiting for, an invitation?" he screamed defiantly. His father had taught him never to go down without a fight, and he was going to honor that advice. He laughed to himself when the grainy image of his drunken father materialized above the hideous expressions leering at him. He imagined his father started scolding him for not looking after his little sister.

"It wasn't my fault dad," he moaned. "Those things took her before I knew what happened." And then the image faded as suddenly as it had come, leaving only the pale faces of the creatures staring at him with hunger in their eyes and black drool dripping from their gaping mouths.

The vampire leader casually strolled over to where the little girl lay on the floor. He bent down next to her as a loving parent would its child, an evil grin plastered across his pale face.

"And now, my dear," he whispered with a wink. "Give me the object. If you do as I say, you may yet die quickly. Otherwise your passing will be most unpleasant, as will your friend's."

The little girl said nothing. She merely looked up into the vampire's snarling face and stared into the soulless, empty eyes. The depth within those eyes was bottomless, like the cold abyss the vampires came from.

"Very well young foolish one," the leader grumbled in disgust. "You have sealed your own fate then. We will have the object soon enough."

The little girl turned her head to one side as if she were actually offering her throat to the fiend. Brad watched, horrified as the huge vampire grinned an impossibly wide smile, from pointed ear to pointed ear, and gripped the little girl's neck in his elongated fingers. Without a sound, and with all of the other vampires looking on, the leader sank his massive, yellowed fangs into her throat.

26

Brad looked past the grotesque faces towering above him to the little girl who was lying on her back with nearly a dozen of the creatures standing above her. The leader apparently had taken his fill, and he slowly stood and sauntered towards the front door. He bumped into a nearby wall and fell to the floor, struggled to stand back up.

Brad wondered if the leader was ill, or better yet, if he were dying. But there were still dozens of other vampires. Too weak to fight, he could only hope that his own death would be quick and painless, although he knew that it probably would not be.

All of the vampires started howling at the top of their lungs. The very walls and ceiling shook from the sheer volume of their cries, dust cascaded down over everything inside the house.

Brad watched as the vampires, which a moment before had appeared to be his impending executioners, fell to the ground. They writhed and twisted in pain unlike anything he had ever seen before. Despite his long-standing hatred for them, he felt a pang of empathy. But only a little one. As soon as he could, he got to his feet and stumbled over to where the little girl lay. She did not move.

"Are you all right?" he asked as he fell to his knees. "Please tell me you're all right.

Please. You have to be."

The little girl opened her eyes and looked up at Brad. Her face was puffed where bruises were already coloring, and her one arm was twisted behind her back in an unnatural way. Brad knew it was definitely broken.

"Do not worry about me," she moaned. "You must take the book out of the house and bury it in consecrated ground. You must smear the pages with holy water. You must believe in its destruction fully, with every fiber in your body and every part of your soul. You must." She pulled the book out from behind her back, and held it out to Brad.

Brad wrenched the book from her hands, and was surprised by just how strong her grip was. It was like trying to take something forcibly from a grown man.

"Was your father really responsible for all this?" he asked. He had to know. He would never be able to rest if he did not know what had caused the terrible holocaust.

"Yes, my father was responsible," the little girl said quietly.

"What's happening to the vampires now?"

"Their race dwelled for eons, knowing that they would have a chance on Earth eventually. All vampires need blood to survive, and each one is linked to another." The little girl paused momentarily, wiped her eyes and then continued.

"After my father realized what he had done,

what the book had used him to do, he set out to remedy the problem. He did manage to complete his work, but did not have time to apply it. The book made it difficult for him to concentrate."

Brad understood about that, now. "But what work did he complete? And what is killing the vampires?" Almost before he finished the sentence, it occurred to him.

It was her blood! The vampire started to die after he drank it.

Brad struggled to speak. "You... were the solution," he whispered. "They started dying after the big one drank your blood."

"My father would have been pleased to know it worked. Humanity is safe."

"Your father," Brad suddenly cried. "We have to go back for him. He could still be alive."

The little girl smiled as best she could. "No, he has passed on. I can feel it. And the house, the book, would make it rather difficult to reach him now."

Brad nodded. The house was still twisting and bending, and the chances of reaching Dr. Vinheiser again were slim. The chasm she had leapt minutes before now nearly split the area they were in from the rest of the house. He stood up and stepped over the remains of the vampires. Most had already been reduced to filthy piles of fine ash, black and acrid, and the ones still alive only faintly resembled the fiendish monsters they had been.

"But how did all of the vampires die if only the leader actually drank your blood?"

"They are all linked to one another," the little girl sighed. "They are all linked..." Her eyes rolled back in her head.

Brad tried to rouse her, then just held her tightly in his arms.

No, no! The pain he felt was only rivaled by the time he lost his little sister. In a way, he had begun to think of the little girl in the same way. Like Amy, she was innocent and frail, too young to survive the horrible affliction that the world faced.

27

Brad struggled to carry her and the book out the front door, but he could not chance leaving either of them behind in the house. He walked between the patches of ichor and ash for a long while before he set her down on the ground, far away from the house. He pulled off what was left of his shirt and wadded it up under her head. She clearly did not need a pillow now, but he thought she would have appreciated the gesture anyway.

Tears of grief and relief streamed down his face as Brad realized he had not asked Dr. Vinheiser the one question he should have. "You willingly sacrificed your life to destroy the vampires, to save us all, and I don't even know your name," Brad sobbed apologetically.

Long after his dehydrated body ran dry of tears, Brad ran out of energy to cry any more, and he stood and looked around what once had been beautiful fields and woods. The dead landscape was littered with the countless remains of the vampires, as far as the eye could see in all directions. Corrupt black dust spilled out of their rotted clothes, grotesque epitaphs to their brief and savage reign.

Brad shuddered as he contemplated the number of fiends that had been waiting outside the house. He realized had Dr. Vinheiser not completed his work, not sacrificed his daughter, there would have been no escape from the house, from the vampires, from any of it.

A gentle but steady wind began to pick up from the east, carrying with it the remains of the vampires far into the horizon. Brad watched the vague, blackish taint in the air as the ashes mingled with the wind. It swirled with the breeze, and could have been beautiful were it not for its nature.

Brad wondered how many people had survived. Surely there must be some others somewhere. He would have to find them, help them, anyway he could. Tell them about *her*, Dr. Vinheiser's solution.

But his first duty was to destroy the book, the curse that unleashed this nightmare in the first place. The little girl had told him how to do it, and he was going to make sure he did, just the way she said. He owed it to her, the old man, himself, the world, to destroy the key to the door between our world and... Brad's blood froze as he realized there could be more fiends, more evil which the book could unleash upon the Earth.

He thought hard and recalled an old church he had passed by before. It had to be about a dozen miles away, but he would find a way to make it there. He remembered how empty it seemed, with nothing but darkness seeping out its foggy, cracked windows. He reluctantly lifted the giant tome, which seemed to be slippery, hard to grip, as the pale promise of sunrise brightened the sky, but did not yet color it.

A shudder ran up his spine when he also recalled how there were some strange noises coming from behind the building, inhuman noises, which sounded like something was being torn apart.

He could only hope that all of the vampires, everywhere, were truly linked with those here.

About the Author

Rick McQuiston is a resident of Warren, Michigan where he enjoys playing drums, horror movies, football, and spending time with family. He is currently employed at Titan Management.

He has over 300 other publications, including *Demonic Visions Vol I, II, III, IV*, two novels, *To See as a God Sees*, and *Where Things Might Walk*, as well as anthology books including *Many Midnights, Chills by Candlelight, Beneath the Moonlight, As Mean as the Night, Cold, Dark Tales, Michigan Madmen, Private Nightmares, Twelve Days of Christmas Horror, Giant Book of Nightmares* and others, which can be found on: Lulu.com, Amazon.com, BarnesandNoble.com.

Visit Many-Midnights.webs.com for more.

Image Credits

Page 6 *geometric motif 2* © Angelo_Gemmi, openclipart.org (modified), public domain

Page 12 *thing* © 2013 rematuche, openclipart.org (modified), public domain

Page 26 detail from *Undead Horizon*, © 2013 Dylan Hansen (modified), used by license

Page 40 *black and white rosette 2* © 2010 Angelo_Gemmi, openclipart.org (modified), public domain

Page 44 detail from *Undead Horizon*, © 2013 Dylan Hansen (modified), used by license

Page 50 *Abstract Liquid Paint Texture* © Madartists | Dreamstime Stock Photos (modified), used per Dreamstime's Limited Royalty Free License terms.

Page 54 *The Signatures of the Seven Demons*, © 1950 Ernst Lehner in Symbols, Signs & Signets of the Dover Pictoral Archive Series, SBN

Page 94   detail from *Undead Horizon*, © 2013
Dylan Hansen (modified), used by
license

Phase 5 considers intellectual property rights a
very serious matter. All our images are used in
accordance with the published or direct
permissions granted by the artists (sometimes
through intermediaries).

We believe in promoting artists and authors
who assist Phase 5 in bringing quality
entertainment to the fans. If you would like to
contact any of these artists, please provide
your information through Customer Service at
www.phase5publishing.com. We will endeavor
to contact the artist or author and relay your
information.

Look for these other Phase 5 Publications:

Sheleasoun: Book I of Beneath the Echoes of Memory by Brandy Wayne

Nerve Zero: A Novel of the Log of The Hand of Tyr by Justin S. Robinson

...The Colour of Time by K. R. Gentile

Dissent: Book I of The Nexus by Thomas Olbert

Scapes, an art anthology

Phase 5 Annual Review, Volume 1, an art and fiction anthology

The Observatory Gardens by James McCarthy

Agents of Paradise by Christopher A. Miller

For more information, visit
www.phase5publishing.com

A Note to the Reader:

Thank you for buying this book, we hope you enjoyed it. You have made the author and artist very happy by validating their talents.

If you enjoyed the book, please let us know (customerservice@phase5publishing.com), and, if you would, publish a review in your venue of choice.

If you did not enjoy it, please let us know what you were expecting that was not delivered in the book (customerservice@phase5publishing.com). Your feedback will help us better design our covers and marketing of this and future publications. We can only meet our goals if we successfully fulfill your expectations.

If you have particular praise or comments regarding the cover art, please send that to us as well, or use the contact information provided at www.phase5publishing.com to let the artist know you appreciate his work.

About the Publisher:

Phase 5 Publishing is dedicated to assisting authors and artists in the science fiction, fantasy and horror genres make their works available to the fans of that genre. We are a small, independent publisher of books in electronic and traditional formats. Formed by fans for fans, we believe that many good pieces of fiction and art need an alternative route to market because they do not fit the popular formula of the day.

We do not discriminate on the basis of the authors' or artists' characteristics (physical, ethnic or other). We judge each work individually, and endeavor to provide useful feedback to submissions that are not accepted so authors and artists can learn from our observations about their works.

We do not accept works that have objectionable subjects or language just for shock value or because it's trendy, but we do accept and publish subjects that may be edgy. We do not publish erotica or content that promotes violence toward or hatred of any person, people, group or classification of people, but our books may contain violence and sexual content, if it serves the story. We endeavor to provide prospective readers full and meaningful information about the book on the cover, so fans know what to expect inside.